Curtain Call

A Play by
Matthew Garlin

Original Concept by
Patrick McCormick & Matthew Garlin

For
Megan and Benjamin

Produced by Acting Out Company Lawrence, MA
Premiered August 9 &10, 2019
Directed by Jodie Putnam

Starring
Mindy Pierce as Pat
Jennifer Onello as Sherri
Anetta Rauf as Amanda
Damien LaCount as Malcolm
Andrew Quinney as Bruce
Lauren Dumont as Joanne

Produced as a Live Zoom Play Reading on August 16th, 2020
Featuring original cast
Directed by Matthew Garlin

AVAILABLE ON THE PODCAST: Everything You Never
Needed to Know about
Movies, Music and Theater available on itunes, castbox, spotify,
anchor and wherever
you get your podcasts.

INTRODUCTION

I began to try to write my own play since I was 15 years old. I had fallen in love
with Neil Simon and Kaufman and Hart and I really wanted to write my own play. I
began by just writing people talking to each other and I lost interest because I hadn't set
up the story. I tried again and I wrote two full plays, but they seemed to be written in the
language of Aaron Sorkin and Tony Kushner. So, I knew I had to try to write about
something else. I did that and the audience really didn't seem to follow it, so I hit reset
and tried again. This is the play that came out.

The characters in this play are loosely based on people from the entire spectrum
of my life and people I worked with when I was doing plays in high school and college
and even now in my professional career. I want to get something across, I am not making
fun of community theater. In fact, I embrace community theater because they embraced
me first. It was a community theater in Reading that took a chance on me as an actor and
gave me a new start and one that I didn't see coming.

This play was actually the second play to get on, but the first play was a staged
reading. This was the first full production play which was produced at Acting out in
Lawrence, MA. I was present at both shows and it was amazing. I had never sat in a
theater and listened to my words being said by actors and actresses who were directed by

a director and I had done nothing except write the words.

A lot of the things in this play are my opinion of the theater in the
past few years
right down to my opinion of huge blockbuster musicals and movie
to musical adaptations
but leaving out the smaller more personal plays which happened to
the movie business
right around the time Jaws and Star Wars came out. I believe that
there is a place in the
business for new original plays in community theater and you
don't have to go to New
York to make a living.

Anyway, this is the first official play that was produced fully, and
it was great.

The cast was great, so much so, that I insisted they do it again
when we did a zoom play
reading during COVID. I hope to see this produced once again and
maybe a theater will
see this potential. I would love to sit in the theater again and watch
actors and actresses
bring this piece to life again.

Enjoy
MATTHEW GARLIN
Matthew Garlin
Playwright

CHARACTERS

Pat – playwright: 26-year-old woman with short hair
Sherri – Producer: 40-year-old practical woman
Amanda – Director: 35-year-old over the top woman

ACTORS
Joanne who ends up playing Sarah
Bruce who ends up playing Jack
Malcolm who ends up playing Ben

ACT ONE

Lights up
The stage has a couch on the far right. A table is to the left with a
notebook on it and five pens and a lamp are right next to it. a chair
is behind the desk as well as three chairs in the foreground. Pat
sits in the chair at the desk as she enters with a latter in her hands.
She opens the notebook and begins to write things down. She stops
every so often and thinks and continues to write as a knock comes
to the door. Pat goes to open it as Sherri enters.

PAT
Come on in.

SHERRI
I better not be wasting my time.

PAT
I'm fine, how are you?

SHERRI
I better not be wasting my time.

PAT
Oh, that's good, I'm glad you're feeling better.

SHERRI
Did you read my notes?

PAT
Yes, my mother is feeling better. Thank you for asking.

SHERRI
Did you read my notes?

PAT

Hip surgery isn't that bad, but I do believe complications can arise.

SHERRI

This was a mistake.

PAT

My dad died from heart complications, but that was his heart, a heart, that's more critical than your hip I'd say, isn't it?

SHERRI

Do you hear yourself?

PAT

I don't know, is the hip attached to anything important?

SHERRI

You're impossible. I am producing your play, a first-time playwright's play, a playwright's first play, the first play of a playwright…

PAT

Is this my first play?

SHERRI

…and you can't even give me a clear answer to my questions. We go on in a month. This isn't summer stock, it's the real deal.

PAT

Why are you talking to me like I don't realize that? What are you worried about?

SHERRI

Your ADD isn't allowing your attention span to last for more than five minutes. I've been here for five minutes and for five minutes, I have been asking you the same question and if my question isn't answered in the next five minutes, I'm leaving and so isn't your production in less than five minutes. So, what do you say to that?

PAT

Can I take five minutes please?

SHERRI

Would you be serious?

PAT

Stop! Okay? I'm twenty-six years old. I've been writing for ten years meaning, I started at sixteen. Meaning, I was putting words on paper when I should have been learning to drive a car or renting a movie or kissing a girl. But I was learning from masters to create worlds on paper for the stage. I watched every play I could see and read every play I could read. We are both pretty smart and we can over come any extra problems we have if there are any. So why don't we take a breath and realize that this is really happening and that, yes, this is my first play produced but the play is solid, and we are going to do great things!

SHERRI

You don't know how to drive a car?

PAT

I know how to ride a bike.

SHERRI

Umm…it's a little bit different.

PAT

Yea, more wheels.

SHERRI

9

Did you read my notes?

PAT
I glanced over them

SHERRI
You glanced over them?

PAT
The vision is more important.

SHERRI
Are you serious… You glanced over them?

PAT
The idea that these two best friends can be split apart by a girl who needs a promotion from one is how it should run, to say nothing about the political farce shit.

SHERRI
You glanced over my notes?

PAT
Why are you repeating everything? Do you think I can't hear you the first time?

SHERRI
I made these suggestions for your benefit. I wanted to give you better idea and to make the play less of a soap opera and more of a drama with some comical elements.

PAT
By changing it to politics and the president? That makes it better?

SHERRI

It's more relevant.

PAT
And more stupid.

SHERRI
Pat...

PAT
Name the first three plays you can think of right now.

SHERRI
What?

PAT
I want you to name the first three plays you can think of right now.

SHERRI
Pat…

PAT
First three plays, right now, go!

SHERRI
Barefoot in the Park, Man who Came to Dinner, and the Mother with the hat.

PAT
Good and what do they have in common.

SHERRI
What?

PAT
What do those three plays you just named have in common?

SHERRI (sarcastic)
Tony Kushner and Aaron Sorkin didn't write any of them.

PAT
No, they all take place in an office or apartment or whatever. No politics in the play and no white house. Why can't we just write about people and what they do in their lives? Why do we need to write complicated shit in the middle of everything? A man grows up and makes a life for himself and happens to meet a girl or a guy and they have a life together. That's it. no politics no complicated shit, just life and reality, reality!

SHERRI
You're doing what then?

PAT
I'm taking a picture of reality.

SHERRI
You should be taking a picture of the picture of reality.

PAT
Why should I be writing far out metaphors that confuse the audience anyway?

SHERRI
Because they sell!

PAT
Years ago, people clamored for real life stories. Now, they want Bretchian epic theater stories about AIDS and the invention of the TV? Even more so, how many movie to musical adaptations are we going to create? Are we really out of ideas that we have to steal from Paddy Chayefsky? Why don't I just write a superhero story,

OH wait, it'll cost 75 million dollars, do you have 75 million dollars for a superhero story? We could add music to it!

SHERRI
I get it, God!

PAT
This play is worth it and if we can get the audience to care about these characters, then they will come. We build it, they will come.

SHERRI
Alright we'll do it your way but when this production fails, you are going to have to explain to your girlfriend and your friends why you can't get a commission from PBS to write a teleplay about spelling.

PAT
You know that this is just community theater, right?

SHERRI
I just want this to work and I want you to get your commission.

PAT
I'm sure I will get the commission and if not, there are always jobs at Dick's Sporting Goods.

SHERRI
Don't kid around. I've seen people greater than you try and fail and then have to go back to their everyday job like Dress Barn.

PAT
Okay here's something things to keep in mind: number 1: it was American Eagle number 2: I got fired from American Eagle for yelling at a woman who couldn't fit in a regular size pants but believed that magic could happen, number 3: I did have a job at

Dick's Sporting Good and the manager told me I could get the job back any time. Number 4: my commission is my own, if people like what I do, fine, but I write for me; no one else, and number five…number 5: do you have 75 million dollars to put on a super hero spectacular rock musical? We can hire a songwriter who writes bland melodies and trite lyrics.

SHERRI
Okay, I get it! (Looks at her watch) Amanda should be here shortly, thank god.

PAT
Why "thank god"?

SHERRI
Because I'm going to take your head and push it throw glass if you keep asking me if I have 75 million dollars to put on a piece of shit.

Pat's demeanor changes as she begins to think about the director coming.

PAT
Is this woman good?

SHERRI
What?

PAT
Amanda?

SHERRI
Yeah?

PAT

Yes Amanda…

SHERRI
What about her?

PAT
Is she good?

SHERRI
Is she good?

PAT
Has this woman directed anything?

SHERRI
She directed traffic!

PAT
Traffic?

SHERRI
She directed traffic.

PAT
At what elementary school? Is she a cop?

SHERRI
Oh no, no, traffic, it was a musical I produced in Gloucester with a
week of performances. This would be her first play.

PAT
Her first play?

SHERRI
Her first stage production without music and dancing.

PAT
You think this is a good idea?

SHERRI
What's a good idea?

PAT
This director who's never directed a play but only musical that is
called Traffic?

SHERRI
You want my opinion? You just tossed my notes away like
yesterdays trash and now you want my opinion?

PAT
Is this a good idea?

SHERRI
Are you getting nervous?

PAT
I am just concerned that a director who hasn't directed anything
except a musical called Traffic is directing my first play. Maybe if
she directed a play called Traffic Jam, I would be confident but…

SHERRI
Would you relax? You know sitting down and taking a nap is not
an occupational hazard in this case. All of the stars are in
alignment and the gods of theater will rein brilliance.

PAT
Who talks like that?

SHERRI

Apparently, I do.

PAT
Sherri…I…

SHERRI
Please! Stay calm. Learn to listen, please. Your ears are attracted to your brain but nothing's going in. You have to trust. Hard. I know, but we all are doing this for one reason. It's a good play. It needs work, but it's a good play. You will not only succeed but thrive because it's a good play. You will be up there so let's climb the mountain and see Zeus.

PAT
Why do you always say that?

SHERRI
What?

PAT
Let's climb he mountain and see Zeus?

SHERRI
It was something my husband always said.

PAT
Really?

SHERRI
Yeah, he was a writer too and he used that has his catchphrase.

PAT
God help me…

SHERRI

He's got his hands full today.

Knock on the door.

SHERRI
Oh, she's here I'll get it. be nice

PAT
I'm always nice.

SHERRI
Just be nice, I'll let her in.

PAT
I'm always nice.

SHERRI
Listen, this woman is interesting, so you know something?

PAT
What?

SHERRI
Be nice, for crying out loud!

PAT
Okay.

SHERRI
And speak slowly.

PAT
Why?

Amanda enters dramatically.

AMANDA
Hello darling!

PAT
Oh my god…

SHERRI
Amanda! Great to see you.

AMANDA
Oh! Such a long day, I could just collapse. Work and more work makes my artistic creative juices run dry. Niagara Falls my creative juices are not but once I sink my teeth into this play, my artistic creative juices runneth over!!

PAT
What the actual f…?

SHERRI
What were they thinking making you work so long, poor dear?

AMANDA
Oh, I shall survive. Ah is this…?

SHERRI
Yes. This is Pat, this is Amanda.

AMANDA
Hello, my boy.

PAT
Boy?

SHERRI

Pat is a…

AMANDA
My boy!

PAT
I'm a woman!

AMANDA
Marvelous play just spectacular I laughed, I cried, and I cried some
more just like after I saw Titanic which I cried at.

PAT
So, you liked it?

AMANDA
Yes, I cried and cried a little more, you know why?

SHERRI
You liked it?

AMANDA
I liked it! But I cried mostly because it's that time.

PAT
What time?

SHERRI
"That" time…

PAT
Oh god!

AMANDA
True to life characters, I say

PAT
So, you liked it?

AMANDA
Absolutely boy!

PAT
Still a woman!

AMANDA
I love it!

SHERRI
She loves it.

AMANDA
I am wild about it.

SHERRI
She's wild about it.

PAT
You loved it?

AMANDA
Amazing play!

SHERRI
She thinks it's an amazing play!

AMANDA
That I do!

PAT

Great!

AMANDA
It does need some work…

PAT
Some work?

SHERRI
She thinks it needs some work.

AMANDA
Needs some work in Act two…

SHERRI
She thinks it needs in Act two…

PAT
I can hear her…

AMANDA
A little tweaking…

SHERRI
No doubt.

AMANDA
And that ending is horrendous!

SHERRI
She doesn't like the ending.

PAT
You didn't like the ending?

AMANDA
It's horrendous!

SHERRI
Terrible!

AMANDA
Agonizing!

SHERRI
No good!

PAT
I get it.

AMANDA
But we'll get to it.

SHERRI
Just takes some time.

PAT
I bet we will.

AMANDA
But I have here…oh now where did I put it, ugh…

Amanda goes looking in her bag as Pat and Sherri go off to the side.

PAT
Does she not realize I'm a woman?

SHERRI
Don't be rude.

PAT
She started it!

Amanda goes in her bag and takes out a phone book of notes.

AMANDA
yes. My notes for a rewrite, boy just some minor details we should
address together as a director to producer to writer.

PAT
These are your notes?

AMANDA
These are my notes.

SHERRI
These are her notes.

PAT
This is a phone book.

AMANDA
No in fact, it's my notes, a phone book, ha! See that's why you're
a writer, you're funny.

PAT
Thanks…

AMANDA
You ever heard of Glengarry Glen Ross?

PAT
My favorite play!

AMANDA
Same amount of notes my boy.

PAT
Same amount of notes?

AMANDA
Same amount of notes.

PAT
Same amount of notes were given to Glengarry Glen Ross as were
given to me.

AMANDA
Indeed, my boy.

PAT
I'm sure Mamet was delighted.

AMANDA
He fired me, but alls well that ends well.

PAT
Right, but…

SHERRI
Let's sit down.

AMANDA
We will get into the writing after today's read through once, we
see what we got.

SHERRI
That's fair

AMANDA
Yes, it is

PAT
It is?

SHERRI
When we see what we got.

PAT
What are the actors like?

AMANDA
The actors?

PAT
Yes, the actors.

SHERRI
They are actors.

PAT
And I'm asking what they are like…

SHERRI
They are great, they are great actors.

PAT
And you know this?

SHERRI
Honestly?

PAT
Yes!

AMANDA
I have no idea!

PAT
Did I ask you?

SHERRI
I hired them.

PAT
And what are they like?

SHERRI
They all have done great plays before I wouldn't worry.

PAT
They have done plays before?

SHERRI
A lot of them.

PAT
And they were good plays?

SHERRI
They were good plays!

PAT
Sherri!

SHERRI
Listen, we have a disadvantage. Every community theater group is
trying to find actors and good ones to put their shows on. It just so

happened when we came around, we got the actors who were left and didn't have jobs yet.

PAT
So, we got the rejects?

SHERRI
We got the actors who weren't right for the other shows but right for our show!

PAT
So, rejects?

AMANDA
Don't worry, my boy, they are my problem, my man. Worry about your words. The words are the gateway into the soul.

PAT
I'm a woman…and aren't those the eyes?

AMANDA
My boy, we have three weeks, so I will do my very best to bring to life your work.

SHERRI
You know Pat actually…

AMANDA
Who's Pat?

PAT
What?

AMANDA
Who is Pat? Is he one of the characters?

PAT
No…

SHERRI
She is.

PAT
Yes…me!

AMANDA
Oh, I am no good with names and nuisance. You know something
people should have name tags on 24/7.

SHERRI
Really?

AMANDA
Name tags! 24/7.

PAT
Right

SHERRI
Anyway, Pat has a great test she gives people to make sure they are
on the same creative page as she is.

AMANDA
Oh really?

SHERRI
Yes

AMANDA
Well my boy, test me.

PAT
Nah, that's okay.

AMANDA
Test me don't be afraid.

PAT
I'm good, I won't test you.

AMANDA
Please test me.

PAT
I'm not going to..,

AMANDA
Test me!

PAT
Okay. Name your three favorite plays right now.

AMANDA
My three favorite…

PAT
Three favorite plays right now.

AMANDA
Oh ha, alright, Coast of Utopia, Angels in America, and A Few
Good Men.

PAT
Okay now what do they have in common?

AMANDA
They are epic plays: politics, religion and human emotion, what plays don't have any of that? Some plays don't even have enough of that.

PAT
Oh god!

AMANDA
Big note for you, boy!

PAT
And here it comes…

SHERRI
You know it!

AMANDA
Politics! Your play is missing that!

PAT
Missing that?

SHERRI
She says your play is missing that.

PAT
Yea, I got that. Amanda, I want to take a picture of reality instead of falling back on a political safe net.

AMANDA
My boy, plays aren't about the picture of reality. Plays are a picture of a picture of reality.

Sherri clears her throat.

AMANDA

My boy, add spice. Well more spice, the play already has some but
add some more my boy. More spice. More seasoning! Basil!
Oregano! Paprika!

PAT

Am I writing a play or making pasta?

AMANDA

My boy, I shall save you. once the actors are here you play will be
mine to capture truth and reality in epic Brecht theater! Victorian
theater! They do some things right!

PAT

God help me!

SHERRI

Pat!

PAT

Please god stay with me.

SHERRI

Pat!

AMANDA

Aristophanes will shine upon you boy. Maybe we should add
music too.

PAT

What?

AMANDA

Music! We should add music!

PAT
Why?

AMANDA
It'll be good!

PAT
When are the actors coming?

SHERRI
Soon…

PAT
Really?

SHERRI
Yes

AMANDA
Add a man hanging from the ceiling,

PAT
Why?

AMANDA
It would be a good visual.

PAT
When?

SHERRI
What?

PAT

When are the actors coming?

SHERRI
Soon!

AMANDA
Maybe even special effects!

PAT
How soon?

AMANDA
Sherri, make room in the budget for explosions and dynamite!
Spare no Expense!

SHERRI
Really?

PAT
What?

AMANDA
Boom! Boom! Blast!

PAT
Where the hell are they?

SHERRI
Who?

PAT
The actors?!

Knock on the door

SHERRI
They are here.

PAT
Thank Christ!

Joanne, Malcolm, and Bruce enter

BRUCE
Nah dude, I passed out first.

MALCOLM
What?

BRUCE
I passed out before you.

MALCOLM
Dude…

BRUCE
I'm saying I passed out before you.

MALCOLM
Yea right. I had so much more Yagar then you did.

BRUCE
You're lying…

MALCOLM
I'm lying?

BRUCE
About having more Yagar than me!

MALCOLM
I did!

BRUCE
You couldn't!

MALCOLM
Why?

BRUCE
Because if you had more Yagar than I did then you would have
passed out before me and I clearly passed out before you.

MALCOLM
I'm saying one thing about that.

BRUCE
What's that?

MALCOLM
I clearly think I had more Yagar than you did because you passed
out first which means that I kept drinking after you passed out like
a woman.

BRUCE
In your dreams.

MALCOLM
That's fine, because if it's in my dream, I am the king of the Yagar
and you are a woman by passing out first.

BRUCE
I'm a woman?

MALCOLM

That's what I'm saying.

JOANNE
Oh, why are the both of you such bros?

BRUCE
I'm a bro?

JOANNE
The two of you are bros.

MALCOLM
We're bros?

JOANNE
You two are such bros!

BRUCE
We are bros, bro…

MALCOLM
Apparently, we are bros, bro!

BRUCE
Nice!

MALCOLM
Awesome!

BRUCE
Kick ass!

MALCOLM
Gnarly!

JOANNE
Will you two shut up?

SHERRI
This is your saving grace.

PAT
Help me!

BRUCE
Dude I will drink you under the mofo table.

MALCOLM
Yea because if you pass out first being a woman that means that
you stop drinking and I can continue drinking more than you can
handle and you want to know why?

BRUCE
Why?

MALCOLM
You're a woman.

JOANNE
Guys!

MALCOLM (making fun of him)
Jo, Bruce is a woman.

JOANNE
Bruce, at what point do you think you have a problem here?

BRUCE

Who? Me?

JOANNE
Yea, you have a problem.

BRUCE
Problems? I have no problems I am a genius, a genius that doesn't
have problems

MALCOLM
That's right, he is not a problem person, he is in fact a genius and
geniuses don't have problems. look at Einstein.

JOANNE
Einstein?

MALCOLM
Einstein, he had no problems.

JOANNE
He was autistic.

MALCOLM
Austistic?

BRUCE (to Malcolm)
That just means he was awesome!

JOANNE
He was awesome?

BRUCE
Einstein was awesome!

MALCOLM

Fucking A!

JOANNE
And Malcolm, where do you come off saying he's a woman? Do you think women can't drink more than men?

MALCOLM
Well no…but…

JOANNE
I could drink you off this planet!

MALCOLM
Yeah…well…I am all that is man!

JOANNE
Oh Lord.

BRUCE
She is speechless.

JOANNE
We dated for 6 years, I've never been speechless in any of those 6 years.

MALCOLM
6 years?

JOANNE
6 years…

MALCOLM
You guys dated for 6 years?

BRUCE

Didn't feel like it?

JOANNE
Oh, thank you!

BRUCE
Felt longer

JOANNE
What?

BRUCE
Nothing

PAT
These are the actors who are the best?

JOANNE (under her breath)
Pig

BRUCE (under his breath)
Slut

PAT
Sherri!

AMANDA
My boy, trust me. The piece will come alive with these individuals putting their stamp on your immortal words.

Bruce belches loudly.

PAT
We are so f-ed.

SHERRI

And you were calm and smart ass-y. Why don't we introduce each
other. I'm Sherri, the producer.

AMANDA

I'm Amanda! I'm the Director but I don't like to think of myself as
a director but as a guider of life and passion.

PAT
What?

SHERRI
Pat, introduce yourself.

PAT
I'm Pat, I'm the playwright.

MALCOLM
You're what?

PAT
I'm the playwright.

MALCOLM
What?

JOANNE

She wrote the play…the reason we are here, the play we were all
cast to be in. She wrote it, you mental midget!

MALCOLM

You wrote these words, dude!!!!!!! That's awesome!! That's like
David Copperfield mind freak awesome!!!! WOO!!!

PAT

My head hurts.

BRUCE
I'm Bruce, man, great job with the play! I'm really excited to play
a mature man.

PAT
Who did you last play?

BRUCE
Oh, I was…well it was The Unexpected Guest.

PAT
That's a great play.

BRUCE
Yea, I was the dead body.

JOANNE
Perfect casting.

BRUCE
Shut up!

JOANNE
Pig!

BRUCE
Slut!

MALCOLM
I am the king.

JOANNE
What?

MALCOLM
I don't need to play it on stage, I am just the king in general.

JOANNE
Yeah, king shit on a turd mountain.

MALCOLM
I'm Malcolm but you can call me awesome!

PAT
Is that your nick name?

MALCOLM
No, I'm just awesome!

BRUCE
Yeah bro!

They high five again.

JOANNE
I'm Joanne, but you can call me Jo and please get me some aspirin.

AMANDA
Now let's take some seats. Out first rehearsal shall be a read through of this immaculate play. Shall we sit?

SHERRI
Let's do…

PAT
Sherri?

SHERRI

Yes?

PAT
I don't think she's using the word immaculate right.

SHERRI
Just let it go.

PAT
Sherri!

SHERRI
Let it go…

AMANDA
Problem?

PAT
Yes…

SHERRI
No! let it go…

AMANDA
So, as we delve into the psyche, we shall begin at the beginning.

SHERRI
Great place to start.

AMANDA
The place to start!

SHERRI
THE place to start

AMANDA
We shall start at the beginning.

PAT
So, let's start!

They all sit down and take out their scripts.

AMANDA
Now Sherri, can you read the stage directions please?

SHERRI
Of course, anyone need anything before we begin?

JOANNE
I need a real man…

BRUCE
I need a real woman…

MALCOLM
Could I get a bagel?

PAT
Let's just start reading please?!

SHERRI
Act one: scene one- lights up. Jack sits in his chair sipping coffee and smoking a pipe, there is a desk on the right side of the stage. Sarah enters.

BRUCE (as Jack)
I thought you were coming right away.

JOANNE (as Sarah)

I did, it's only been an hour.

JACK
It's been three.

SARAH
Are you sure?

JACK
I have eyes, I have a watch, I know how to use them both, it's been
three hours since I left you.

SARAH
I wanted to stay longer.

JACK
You didn't seem to be having a fun time when we were there
together.

SARAH
I had a good time.

JACK
You didn't look like it.

SARAH
I did

JACK
Really?

SARAH
Yes

JACK

And you were talking to Ben.

SARAH
So?

JACK
you were talking to Ben...

SARAH
Yes...

JACK
Ben was talking with you…

SARAH
That's how it works…

JACK
You do know Ben is a colleague who I'm in competition with right?

SARAH
Ben? Are you asking me about Ben?

JACK
I am and I want to know why you spent three hours talking to Ben.

SARAH
I have been friends with Ben for fifteen years. Why would I talk to him for three hours when I could talk to him for four hours? Is that what you're asking?

JACK
No! I am asking why you are talking to Ben, my only competition for the executive job that I rightfully deserve and have worked

twenty years to get by now but may be passed over for it because Huckleberry Finn wants to help his friend Jim cross the Mississippi instead of helping me, Tom Sawyer, get a merger. Ben is a man who would rather start a new project with China rather than invest in an Indian company. Why would you talk about anything to Ben, my mortal enemy who may make millions of dollars instead of me for three hours when you should barely give him a minute of your time? That's what I'm asking.

SARAH
Are you jealous of Ben?

JACK
Go to bed.

SARAH
No, answer me

JACK
Put your head to rest.

SARAH
Answer me!

JACK
I forgot the question.

SARAH
Are you jealous of Ben?

JACK
What?

SARAH

You are! You want to answer but your mind makes you wonder if you know what you feel is true. Your mouth and mind deceive you far beyond what you are comfortable admitting. Maybe you should realize how I made a vow to you and your name. trust is something I ask from you, but you don't know how to give it. You've spent your time cutting people's throats and now you don't know how to believe coherent words coming out of my mouth, do you? do you?

JACK
Go to bed!

SHERRI
A knock comes to the door as Ben enters.

MALCOLM (as Ben)
Great party tonight.

SARAH
Please leave us alone.

BEN
I wanted to tell you what I thought of the party.

JACK
Get out, fucker!

BEN
That's a mite harsh, am I interrupting something?

SARAH
Kind of...

JACK
Yes!

BEN
Oh, did you tell him, Sarah?

SARAH
Shut up!

JACK
What? Tell me what?

SARAH
Not now!

BEN
Sarah and I are in love…

JACK
What?

SARAH
He's…he's drunk.

BEN
I came back to get your blessing and give her a ring.

JACK
What?

SARAH
Funny joke, Ben.

JACK
I'll kill you both.

SARAH
Baby…

JACK

Don't baby me! I will beat you both dead with a stapler.

BEN

It's good to see you're taking this so well.

JACK

Go fuck yourself.

SHERRI

Jack lungers for Ben as Sarah screams as we see Jack beat Ben up.

MALCOLM

Hold on, hold on, so I don't fight back at all?

PAT

What? When?

MALCOLM

Now?! I'm not fighting him; I'm being attacked?

PAT

Yea…

MALCOLM

Yea?

PAT

Why?

MALCOLM

Okay, he's the badass and I'm the bitch, and what part should I not
be insulted by?

PAT
This is the character…

MALCOLM
Dude…

PAT
This is the character!

BRUCE
You're a woman!

PAT
Your character…

JOANNE
Oh, shut up about the whole being a woman thing!

PAT
Your character is more of a lover than a fighter.

BRUCE
What?

PAT
His character…

MALCOLM
What the hell?

JOANNE
True to life characters.

PAT
His character is the lover, you're the fighter.

JOANNE
Perfect casting.

BRUCE
Excuse me!

PAT
Let's keep going.

BRUCE
Wait, can I make a statement?

SHERRI
Let's keep going.

JOANNE (laughing)
Mine is an hysterical laugh

PAT
You guys should stop talking you know why?

BRUCE
Why?

PAT
Because we should continue reading the goddamn play!

SHERRI
Can we keep going please?

BRUCE (to Joanne)
You saying I have no feelings?

JOANNE

I just said perfect casting, you make your own interpretation.

MALCOLM
But why do I have to get my ass kicked?

PAT
Because…

MALCOLM
Why am I getting an ass kicking?

PAT
It's in the script, it's there in the script. Right here in the script, didn't you read the script?

MALCOLM
Yea, but I didn't read "Ben gets the shit kicked out of him cause he's a Nancy bitch to Jack's Rambo".

SHERRI
Read, please!

BRUCE
Keep your comments to yourself, Jo!

JOANNE
Uh hello, free country.

BRUCE
You can take your Bill of Rights and…

PAT
Let's read the fucking play!!

AMANDA

Ha! I have it! I've got the greatest theatrical idea ever posed on a theater.

Long Pause

PAT
Yes? Are we going to hear it or are you keeping it to yourself?

AMANDA
They are both lovers and fighters!

PAT
What?

AMANDA
They are both lovers and fighters!

PAT
I heard you the first time I'm just saying…that's not the story! They are opposites; you can't have two of the same kind of characters, one is one way the other is another way, that's how drama works!

AMANDA
What if they were aliens?

Pat hits her head on her desk.

PAT
Aliens?

AMANDA
And they copied each other's traits!

PAT

What?

SHERRI
Pat?

AMANDA
Each other's traits

PAT
Aliens?

AMANDA
What's wrong, my boy?

SHERRI
It's an interesting idea, Pat

PAT
First of all, I am a woman not a "boy" and secondly, this isn't Close Encounters nor I Robot nor any other science fiction film, it's a dramatic play about two friends who get torn apart by a girl told backwards. It's not about aliens or robots.

AMANDA
But it can be!

PAT
What?

AMANDA
We can be unlike any other play every produced. We can be the changing play. Ambition?!

PAT
You do know this is community theater and not Broadway.

AMANDA
We need a start.

PAT
Amanda?!

AMANDA
My boy! Theater is a living breathing animal and we are meant to worship it like it is a living breathing animal. There are things we don't understand like living breathing animals and there are things that we do understand.

PAT
And theater is one of those things?

AMANDA
Yes!

PAT
And so, our characters are going to be the same?

AMANDA
Yes!

PAT
Why?

AMANDA
Because theater is a living…

PAT
Living breathing thing

AMANDA

Animal!

PAT
Sherri please do something!

SHERRI
Why don't we take a five minute break?

Everyone starts to leave.

PAT
This is going to be so long.

Lights down

END OF ACT ONE

ACT TWO

*Lights up. Setting is the theater. There is an arm chair with a
coffee table in front and an end table next to the arm chair. There
is a desk on the left side of the room. Bruce sits in the chair. It's
the play they are performing. Bruce is dressed in a smoking jacket
while he has an bionic eye patch. Joanne enters in a catsuit with a
corset around her waist and a fake red head wig on. She is holding
a whip in her right hand. Amanda is in the audience watching and
whispering suggestions while Pat and Sherri are in the tech booth.*

BRUCE (as Jack)
I thought you were coming right away.

JOANNE (as Sarah)
I did, it's only been an hour, darling

JACK
It's been three.

SARAH
Are you sure?

JACK
I have eyes, I have a watch, I know how to use them both,
especially with this bionic eye which can shoot lasers outwards
toward you. It's been three hours since I left you.

SARAH
I wanted to stay longer.

JACK
You didn't seem to be having a fun time when we were there
together.

SARAH
I had a good time.

JACK
You didn't look like it.

SARAH
I did.

JACK
Really?

SARAH
Yes

JACK
And you were talking to Ben.

SARAH
So?

JACK
you were talking to Ben.

SARAH
Yes.

JACK
Ben was talking with you

SARAH
That's how it works unless I use my telepathic algorithm machine.

JACK

You do know Ben is a colleague who I'm in competition with right?

SARAH

Ben? Are you asking me about Ben?

JACK

I am and I want to know why you spent three hours talking to Ben.

SARAH

I have been friends with Ben for fifteen years and was a lover of for 9 of those years. Why would I talk to him for three hours when I could talk to him for four and be with him for an extra hour for the right price if you know what I mean, darling? Is that what you're asking?

JACK

No! I am asking why you are talking to Ben, my only competition for the executive job that I rightfully deserve and have worked twenty years to get by now but may get passed over because Huckleberry Finn wants to help his android friend Jim go to the Mississippi Plant instead of helping me, Tom Sawyer, get a merger. Ben is a man who would rather start a new project with Planet China 1138 rather than invest in the Tyrel Industry. Why would you talk about anything to Ben, my mortal enemy who may make trillions of dollars in stead of me for three hours when you should barely give him a minute of your time? That's what I'm asking.

SARAH

Are you jealous of Ben?

JACK

Go to bed.

SARAH
No, answer me.

JACK
Put your head to rest and take your battery out, they don't grow on
trees, which are scarce now.

SARAH
Answer me!

JACK
I forgot the question.

SARAH
Are you jealous of Ben?

JACK
What?

SARAH
You are! You want to answer but your mind makes you wonder if
you know what you feel is true which makes sense since the aliens
took over our planet. Your mouth and mind deceive you far
beyond what you are comfortable. Maybe you should realize how I
made a vow to you and your name and your robotic ligaments.
trust is something I ask from you, but you don't know how to give
it. You've spent your time cutting people's throats with your alien
claws and now you don't know how to believe coherent words
coming out of my mouth and my electronic voice box, do you? do
you?

JACK
Go to bed!

Malcolm comes in with a gigolo outfit with his shirt half off and tentacles coming out of his ass.

MALCOLM (as Ben)
Great party tonight.

SARAH
Please leave us alone.

BEN
I wanted to tell you what I thought of the party.

JACK
Get out, fucker!

BEN
That's a mite harsh, am I interrupting something?

SARAH
Kind of

JACK
Yes.

BEN
Oh, did you tell him Sarah?

SARAH
Shut up!

JACK
What? Tell me what?

SARAH
Not now!

BEN
Sarah and I are in love

JACK
What?

SARAH
He's…he's drunk.

BEN
I came back to get your blessing and give her this galactic ring
forged from Jupiter's moons.

JACK
What?

SARAH
Funny joke, Ben.

JACK
I'll kill you both.

SARAH
Baby.

JACK
Don't baby me! I will beat you both dead with electronic magnetic
newspaper.

BEN
It's good to see you're taking this so well.

JACK
Go fuck yourself

Jack lunges toward Ben as Sarah tries to pull them off each other. Jack punches Ben who then punches Jack back as Sarah punches Jack and Jack punches Ben again and kisses Sarah as Sarah punches Ben and Ben punches Jack.

Amanda comes forward.

AMANDA
No, no, no she slaps him then he slaps him then she chokes him then he bites her then he sucker punches him and he kisses her, got it?

BRUCE
What?

AMANDA
She slaps him then he slaps him then she chokes him then he bites her then he sucker punches him and he kisses her, got it?

MALCOLM
I got it

JOANNE
You don't think it's over doing it?

BRUCE
I can't even remember my lines never mind punching or kissing everyone.

AMANDA
What's so hard to remember it's: she slaps him then he slaps him then she chokes him then he bites her then he sucker punches him and he kisses her, got it?

BRUCE
Oh, I punch him and kiss her?

AMANDA
Yes!

BRUCE
Oh okay, because I've been punching her and kissing him, and I
thought that was kind of odd.

AMANDA (losing her patience)
Yes! She slaps him then he slaps him then she chokes him then he
bites her then he sucker punches him and he kisses her, got it?

PAT (OS)
Oh my god!

SHERRI (OS)
Shut up…

AMANDA
Problem?

PAT(OS)
Holy shit balls!

SHERRI (OS)
Please stay seated…

AMANDA
Problem?

SHERRI (OS)
No, no, don't worry

AMANDA
Let us continue then.

JOANNE
Can I ask a question?

AMANDA
What?

JOANNE
Why do I look like a dominatrix?

AMANDA
What?

JOANNE
Why do I look like a dominatrix?

AMANDA
Because…

JOANNE
Theater is a living breathing…

AMANDA
Theater is a living breathing animal!!

JOANNE
Okay so after rehearsal I'll go just around the corner and become a prostitute.

BRUCE
Only way someone would actually sleep with you.

JOANNE

Pig!

BRUCE
Slut!

AMANDA
Okay! let's continue.

Pat runs up on stage followed by Sherri.

PAT
No, why don't we answer that question.

AMANDA
What?

SHERRI
Pat….

PAT
Please, let's answer the question.

AMANDA
My boy, we must not question creativity.

PAT
Creativity?

AMANDA
What?

BPAT
Creativity? Creativity yes, but outrageous ideas that don't work is
another thing.

AMANDA

My boy, the night before an opening night is not a great time to start asking creative questions, that's what rehearsal days are for.

PAT

Well you interrupt me anytime I try to ask something else so why wouldn't I make it known right before its too late.

AMANDA

Unprofessionalism, that's why this is. I'm taking on your piece of shit work and you have the nerve to question me?

PAT

You said you liked it.

AMANDA

You said you'd work on it.

PAT

You said you liked it!

AMANDA

My boy

SHERRI

Pat?!

PAT

She said she liked the play.

AMANDA

My boy

PAT

You just called in a piece of shit play.

SHERRI
Pat?!

PAT
She called my play that I spent working on for three years a piece
of shit play.

SHERRI
Okay, why don't we take a break?

JOANNE
Guys, seriously all I want to know is why am I dressed like a
dominatrix.

BRUCE
I'm not complaining!

JOANNE
You pig!

SHERRI
Okay, five minutes everyone let's cool off.

PAT
I just want to know…

SHERRI
Pat?!

AMANDA
I need to take a minute away; my creative juices are flowing but
the questions that you all are posing are draining the well. I need to
squeeze more fruit and get some creative juices flowing again!

PAT (To Sherri)
Seriously? What the actual f...?

Amanda leaves dramatically everyone walks around before finding a place to sit.

BRUCE
Ahh just another day.

MALCOLM
How am I doing?

BRUCE
It's tough.

MALCOLM
I was actually talking to her.

BRUCE
What?

MALCOLM
I was talking to Joanne.

BRUCE
Why?

MALCOLM
Why?

BRUCE
Why were you asking Joanne that question?

MALCOLM
What?

JOANNE
Mal…

BRUCE
Why were you asking Joanne how you're doing?

MALCOLM
I'm asking…

JOANNE
Mal!

BRUCE
Are you two dating??

SHERRI
We should let you guys be, Pat?

PAT
Are you kidding me? This is more interesting than the Red Sox
playing the Yankees!

BRUCE
You guys are dating?!

MALCOLM
Bud…

BRUCE
You guys ARE dating?!

MALCOLM
Yea!

JOANNE
Bruce…

BRUCE
Why are you guys dating?!

MALCOLM
Bruce…

JOANNE
I swear to God, Bruce, that I wouldn't even tell you anything about
our situation if you were a priest in a confessional.

BRUCE
Oh my god! When did you two start dating?

JOANNE
None of your business!

BRUCE
When did you two start dating?!

MALCOLM
Two months ago.

JOANNE
Don't tell him!

MALCOLM
Two months ago, we started dating!

JOANNE
These two morons don't know how to listen to a woman when a
woman is talking.

BRUCE
If there were a woman standing here that was worth listening to, I
might actually hear what she says.

JOANNE
Screw you!

BRUCE
Two months ago?

MALCOLM
Yea, two, right, hunny?

JOANNE
I'm done with both of you right now.

BRUCE
Two months ago?!

MALCOLM
Exactly!

JOANNE
Here it comes…

BRUCE
That was before we started rehearsals, wasn't it?

MALCOLM
Umm…

BRUCE
That was before we started rehearsals, wasn't it?

JOANNE

Yes, it was, so what?

BRUCE
So…so we've been hanging out, getting drunk and high while you
were dating with my girlfriend?

JOANNE
Ex-girlfriend…

BRUCE
What?

MALCOLM
No! of course not! We didn't start till a week after we started
rehearsals.

BRUCE
After we started rehearsals?

MALCOLM
After...

PAT
Oh, and this is getting good.

JOANNE
Bruce…

BRUCE
I'm surprised at you. not you Jo, you were always a lying bitch
from the moment you walked into my dorm and asked to use a
phone after you left your boyfriend's room after a very loud and
vocal argument that everyone on the quad could hear.

JOANNE

Oh, you're really doing this all over again.

BRUCE
Jo!

JOANNE
Bruce, I got something to tell you about that night, he was drunk
and trying to have his way with me, and I got out of his way that
night and I thank god because he passed out in the middle of a
football field. I came into your dorm because I needed someone
and instead of holding me like you should have, you decided to
make fun of me during that entire first meeting,

BRUCE
And yet you stayed!

Joanne goes silent.

BRUCE
I'm not surprised at all, Jo. But you, Mal, what about our
friendship?

MALCOLM
What do you mean?

BRUCE
Our code? The friendship code?

MALCOLM
What code?

BRUCE
The friendship code. It's in the book of friendship

MALCOLM

There's a friendship book?

BRUCE
Yes!

MALCOLM
What friendship code and what is this book?

BRUCE
The code of friendship! No dating ex-girlfriends! Rule 203, Rule 203, there's a rule 203 of not dating ex-girlfriends, Malcolm!

JOANNE
Okay, how juvenile can you be?

BRUCE
Out of all the people here right now, I think you should be the last one to talk.

JOANNE
Seriously

BRUCE
Apparently as juvenile as you are, Jo

JOANNE
I don't make up random rules and I don't hold bitter grudges, so I think you're at a lower level than me when it comes to anything like that.

MALCOLM
Dude, we've been friends for years and I don't remember…is there really a rulebook with 202 in writing?

JOANNE

He said it was 203 and no, he's playing with you.

MALCOLM
I trust him enough; can I buy it at Barnes and Noble or something?

JOANNE
Shut up!

BRUCE
You two have turned on me?!

JOANNE
Are you serious?

BRUCE
Trust broken by two former friends!

JOANNE
Are you serious?

MALCOLM
Dude, come on, tell me where I can purchase that book, I'll read it, honest I will.

PAT
This is better than Netflix.

BRUCE
Who knew two friends could break a trust strong enough to last a hurricane?

JOANNE
You can not be serious.

BRUCE

Oh, for crying out loud, what do you want me to say?

MALCOLM
Can I get it on my kindle?

JOANNE
You're jealous!

BRUCE
What?

JOANNE
You are jealous!

BRUCE
Are you serious…oh you got me doing it now?

MALCOLM
Is the book in paperback or do I need to buy the hardcopy version?

JOANNE
Shut up! For the love of God, shut up. You two are sleezy slimey oversexed addle minded mongrels with the sensitivity of a head of cabbage.

BRUCE
The hell does that mean?

JOANNE
That means that you're a piece of shit both of you!

MALCOLM
Well you're a poopy head!!

JOANNE

A poopy head?

MALCOLM
Yeah, I'm not as good with comebacks are you are English College
Alumni!

JOANNE
I didn't go English college. I went to college for English where I
took courses for English and I am able to converse in English and
you two took classes in I don't even know what.

BRUCE
Women studies.

JOANNE
You took classes in women studies?

BRUCE
I graduated with a degree in women studies

JOANNE
You have a degree in women studies? You? you of all the people
in the world, you have a degree in women studies?

BRUCE
Yea, I really am quite something.

JOANNE
I can't believe you.

BRUCE
I can't believe that after the pain in the ass time I gave you the first
time I met you, you decided not only to stay but date me for 6
years afterwards.

JOANNE
Well I was in love with you!!

BRUCE
What?!

JOANNE
Even though, you sat there and made fun of me at first night, I found out later that it's your way to make someone feel better. You were trying to make me feel better. We started to hang out more and I developed a crush which lead to actually having feelings for you! It all came crashing down but that doesn't mean that I stopped feeling things for you. I fell in love with you because you made me feel better but then later when it turned to hurtful words, I decided to walk away. There you happy! That's the secret I've been keeping. You constantly calling me names is why I left. What do you think about those apples? Where is that in your friendship/ bro code book?

Amanda enters

AMANDA
Okay, back to work…

PAT
Ugh! It was getting good.

MALCOLM
I swear if it's the last thing I do…

AMANDA
Let's go back to it, my boy.

MALCOLM
I'm going to find that book, I swear to God I am going to.

AMANDA

Come on, we must get this on its feet. Now comes the big explosions.

PAT

Please, tell me you mean in terms of a dramatic climax

AMANDA

No I mean…blast!!

A big explosion comes about…

PAT

Holy shit!

AMANDA

There you go!

PAT

What was that?

JOANNE

That was loud

MALCOLM

I just soiled myself

PAT

You put charges in a theater.

SHERRI

Those were only the first ones.

MALCOLM

I pooped in my pants

PAT
Wait there is more?

SHERRI
Six more charges

PAT
Why do we need any explosions?

AMANDA
Climax dramatics.

MALCOLM
Okay, I seriously need a new pair of pants because I just shat myself. (*Exits*)

JOANNE
What? Does this look like Macy's Thanksgiving Day Parade?

SHERRI
She put in explosions last night.

PAT
I still don't understand…why?

SHERRI
For climax…

PAT
If I hear that answer one more time, I swear to God I'm going to attack someone.

SHERRI

People will buy a ticket to see explosions.

PAT
Why?

SHERRI
Because they bought tickets to see Transformers

PAT
They bought tickets to see Transformers because of Megan Fox and her boobs. Michael Bay is the worst example for why money happens to come into play with art. He doesn't do art, he does spectacle.

SHERRI
Spectacle sells!

Malcolm re-enters

AMANDA
Wait until we get to the interracial-species sex scene

PAT
Look, I can understand the money situation, but this is…wait what?!

AMANDA
The interracial…

PAT
We have a sex scene in the play?

SHERRI
We do

PAT
I didn't write a sex scene in the play!

SHERRI
You did not…

AMANDA
I wrote it for the play last night, my boy. You needed some color,
some sex!

PAT
They are going to have sex. (Referring to Joanne and Bruce)

AMANDA
No, he is.

BRUCE
I get to fuck a goat!

PAT
Where does it say that?

MALCOLM (very proud)
I get to fuck a porcupine.

JOANNE
How did I find these morons attractive at all?

SHERRI
Sex sells!

AMANDA
Also, Bruce, his character should be killed at the end.

PAT

Why?

AMANDA
He should die!

JOANNE
I'll go with that.

PAT
Why?

BRUCE
It'll be dramatic and poignant.

PAT
He's the hero, he can't die.

SHERRI
Death sells also.

PAT
Is that why she's in a dominatrix outfit and why there are spaceship flying around behind and is that why I have a stomachache about all of this?

SHERRI
This stuff sells that's why we are using them.

AMANDA
My boy…

PAT
Sherri!

AMANDA

My boy…

PAT
Sherri!

AMANDA
Shut up! Now, I've been listening to your smug out bursts and so now, it's my turn. Now, not for nothing, but Someone must level with you. your play is boring. We are amping the temperature up to a Fahrenheit level so that we can butts in the seats. Explosions, exotic costumes and sex are the only ways I know how to get people into the theater and although I don't really give a shit what you think of me, I have my name on this play and I'm going to do this the best I can do it so get on board, my boy!

PAT
Really?

JOANNE
And Bruce is a horrible actor who should always get killed on a stage any chance he can.

BRUCE
Screw you!

JOANNE
Already did, wasn't that great the first time.

MALCOLM
I was better?

JOANNE
Not by much

BRUCE

You two slept together?

JOANNE
That's what almost always happens between two people who are
dating, genius.

MALCOLM
Yea, we did it, man, I totally tapped that. High five!

Malcolm goes in for a high five as Bruce just stares at him.

BRUCE
You slept with her…

MALCOLM
Yes, I did, High five!

BRUCE
Wow…

JOANNE
You dated after we broke up

BRUCE
I didn't sleep around with random women and I didn't sleep with
your best friend, big difference!

JOANNE
Really?

BRUCE
Yes!

JOANNE
I had heard you did. That was the only thing that broke us up.

BRUCE

NO! I didn't sleep with your best friend. Nina is just a raging liar.

JOANNE

You're telling the truth?

BRUCE

Oh, wow I told a truth! That's shocking, I know! Let's cry about it!

JOANNE

I didn't know…I'm sorry

BRUCE

Now, you do and now, I do. Now, I have to live with that.

(Awkward Pause)

MALCOLM

Yea, I gave it my all, buddy, high five!

BRUCE

Goddamnit! I'm not going to give you a high five. You slept with this woman who I dated for six years and you betrayed friendship code 203, 204 and 205, how do you feel about yourself now?

MALCOLM

Buy me the book so I can learn about these rules, man!

SHERRI

Okay, okay, enough of this! let's get back to work.

PAT

Oh yea, that's a great idea…

SHERRI
Pat?

Pat starts to walk out.

SHERRI
Pat!

AMANDA
My boy, come back, we must finish rehearsing your play

PAT
My play? My play?

AMANDA
Yes, my boy!

PAT
This is not my play. My play is about a love triangle that ends up
in sadness with the girl crying. My play is steeped in cynical irony
and my play is realistic enough that the audience will believe they
are living in their own lives and are trying to figure out their own
lives while the play is on that stage. There are no explosions in my
play. There is no death in my play and there are no sex scenes with
a goat and a llama in my play.

MALCOLM
It's a porcupine

PAT
What?

MALCOLM
It's a porcupine, I'm fucking a porcupine

Pat flips the desk over and throws things around.

PAT
What the hell? I don't care! There are no dominatrix outfits, spaceships, or any other bull shit. It's a simple play where those who are working on it have an attention span higher than a moron with a potato gun. They love theater and they want to do this play and don't have personal arguments all through the rehearsals. That's the play experience I want. I want them to not worry about what sells and I want them to talk to me like I'm a playwright and not like I'm five years old and doing my first Christmas pageant. I have been writing for 10 years and I spent 5 of those years learning about theater in college as well as seeing every play and every musical I could on Broadway and off. I have had my work reviewed by theater directors in my schools and I am never ever sick at sea. So do your play now. do YOUR play. This is not my play, I'm not proud of this play at all and even having my name in the margins of the footnotes for this one makes me want to throw up profusely. A monkey could do a better job at this play right now and guess what? I'm no monkey and this is not my play.

Pat walks to the edge of the stage as Sherri stops her.

SHERRI
Could everyone step out for a second? Take a five-minute break. I'd like to talk to Pat privately please.

They all leave one at a time. Sherri sits next to Pat on the edge of the stage.

SHERRI
So…

PAT
Don't say it!

SHERRI
I just said so…

PAT
Don't say it!

SHERRI
I just said so would you calm down?

PAT
You're going to say it. I know you are going to say it. well you
know what I don't want to hear it.

SHERRI
You realize she's only trying to help…

PAT
With bad ideas? How are bad ideas going to help this play? My
first play? Bad ideas are not going to help this play. Oh, and by the
way, it's my first play!

SHERRI
They aren't bad ideas.

PAT
You're right, chasing a squirrel into a tree full of killer bees, that's
a bad idea, these ideas are horrible. I'm talking Carrot Top
Comedy Bad!

SHERRI
Why don't you give it a chance?

PAT
Because it's wrong!

SHERRI
It's wrong?

PAT
Yea it's just wrong!

SHERRI
I don't believe…

PAT
What?

SHERRI
I don't believe right and wrong goes into stagecraft!

PAT
You don't? you don't think right and wrong go into stagecraft
because I think you'll full of shit.

SHERRI
Yea, piss off your producer, that's a great idea just like that killer
bee idea

PAT
Sherri…

SHERRI
No, I don't think right and wrong go into stage craft; this isn't
world peace, this isn't democracy or any kind of peace agreement,
this is theater! It's entertainment. Right and wrong don't enter
stage craft but you know what does?

PAT
What?

SHERRI
Creation and creativity!

PAT
What in god's name…

SHERRI
Creation and creativity!

PAT
What are we gods?

SHERRI
You know what? Yea, we are. We are gods creating worlds out of
thin air. We are putting grass, trees and buildings where there were
no grass, trees and buildings. We are putting people in those
worlds where they had been non-existent before. We are using
whatever creativity we have to put a world in front of an audience
that is new and different. Why because we are new and different,
and we have good ideas. Sometimes those ideas end up being bad
but sometimes they turn out to be good, but who are we to know
unless we go down that road and put it in front of an audience?
(Pause) Is that what you didn't want me to say?

PAT
But why does it have to sell?

SHERRI
Because...you love this, don't you?

PAT
Yes, I do

SHERRI

Well, let me tell you a story: There was a man a long time ago who loved theater too, and he thought outside the box like you. But he didn't know how to have the audience relate to what he was doing on stage. He didn't realize how paramount that was. He spent every last dime he had on this new play by a new playwright– All of his savings… He bet the farm on it. The audience didn't buy into any of his ideas and the world he created disappeared into thin air. That was the key, because you can be as experimental as you want. You can have good ideas and bad ideas. But, if an audience can't buy any of those ideas, then what you have just disappears- like his world. He had good ideas, but he also didn't know how to present them. He was so depressed and lost, he decided to jump off the Golden Gate Bridge (Pause) I want this to sell and I want the audience to buy this. I don't want YOUR world to disappear into thin air. YOU can do MORE - More creating, more worlds with grass, trees and buildings and many more worlds out of thin air. Do you know what I'm saying?

PAT
So what do we do?

SHERRI
We ride it out, all we can do is try. Nothing more; nothing less. Good ideas, bad ideas, they are ideas. Take the porcupine and the goat and the death and explosions and see if it connects with the audience. Do you think on the 6th day when God created the earth, he thought porcupine was a bad idea? He could have killed it off right away; he was God anyway. Pride of what he created, that's what you need.

PAT
I didn't create this!

SHERRI
You…you wrote this.

PAT
Not like this?!

SHERRI
Do you think they've done Shakespeare the same way every time?
Directors put spins on them and sometimes they spin too much but
you have to let them spin the creativity. It's about respect of
creativity. You're not the only one with a creative bone in your
body.

PAT
Do you think the play is good?

SHERRI
Pat…

PAT
Do you think the play's good?!

SHERRI
I don't think…

PAT
Is the play good?!

SHERRI
Without all the bullshit, yes.

PAT
Then what are we waiting for?

SHERRI

What if I lost you something you love dearly? I'm trying to make it commercial so you have a job next month and you can quit you job at Starbucks.

PAT
Dress Barn…

SHERRI
Whatever…

PAT
That's what you're worried about?

SHERRI
Pat…

PAT
What are you worried about me for?

SHERRI
Because you love theater and like me you want to be able to make a living from theater and the water under the Golden Gate Bridge is freezing cold.

(Pause)

PAT
Alright, Sherri, good idea, bad idea, let's create. Tomorrow is the 7th day so we can rest. Let's make the porcupine tonight.

They hug

SHERRI
Alright, let's get back to work.

PAT
Sherri?

SHERRI
Yea?

PAT
Who was that guy?

SHERRI
What guy?

PAT
The golden gate bridge guy.

SHERRI
My husband…

(Pause)

PAT
I'm sorry…

SHERRI
He did it after a play I wrote for him. He fell in love with it. The difference is I'm not a playwright, you are, and he would be proud of you.

PAT
Really?

SHERRI
I'm inclined to think he'd like your play

PAT

Really?

SHERRI
Yea

PAT
And the changes?

SHERRI
He would have kept the death scene, but I would hope he'd cut the porcupine sex scene.

PAT
Smart guy. He had some good ideas, he was with you.

Amanda, Joanne, Malcolm and Bruce enter

AMANDA
My boy.

PAT
Alright, Amanda, let's get back to work.

AMANDA
I have thought it over and I apologize. Cut the special effects, cut the sex scene and cut the death scene.

PAT
No, keep the death scene.

BRUCE & JOANNE
Yes!

AMANDA
And the sex scene?

PAT
Hell no!

MALCOLM
Does this mean?

AMANDA
Boys, you need to be in the suits, Joanne, you need to change out
of the dominatrix outfit and if I see the porcupine anywhere, I'll
beat the person who left it there in the face with it.

JOANNE
Yes!!

BRUCE
Aww

JOANNE (more gentle)
Pig!

BRUCE (more lovingly)
Jo!

MALCOLM
So, I don't need this lube anymore?

AMANDA
Come one ladies and gentlemen we have a play to do.

PAT
We are gods and we have one more day before we can rest.

MALCOLM
I never get to do anything I want to…

Everyone gets to their places as Sheri puts her arm around Pat who looks ecstatic.

Lights down

END OF ACT 2

ACT THREE

Lights up
The stage opens as it has at the beginning of Act one. There is a stack of papers on the desk. Everything is calm. Bruce, Joanne, and Malcolm enter in jubilance.

MALCOLM
Oh my God

JOANNE
We did it!

MALCOLM
Oh my god

BRUCE
Wow!

MALCOLM
Oh my god

JOANNE
I can't believe we did it.

MALCOLM
Oh my god!

JOANNE
Bruce please say…Malcolm stop…okay Bruce you're just standing there, say something, say something, Bruce say something please and Malcolm come up with something cleverer than "oh my god".

MALCOLM

Oh my…Buddha!

JOANNE
Bruce, for crying out loud say something! Use your words! All he can fucking say is "oh my god", the least, at the very least, you must have something more articulate and intelligent a response than "oh my god" guy over here. I want to hear the words from you. from your mouth I want to hear the words from you that you are proud, elated, pissed off, any of the above. Poets and lyricists spend a lot of time to come up with the right word to describe their situation. I am giving you exactly until the end of this sentence to say at least something. It doesn't have to be worth publishing but just something that describes how you are feeling right now. Now please speak. As Taylor Swift would say, speak now!

BRUCE
Wow…

JOANNE
You really dropped the ball right there. I was expecting so much more of you! I mean if you could just say one thing…I gave you a chance to be articulate and explain yourself. You could have used Shakespeare or Aristotle, or fucking Mamet and you couldn't even come up with one thing that would describe your…

Bruce screams loudly and very crazy as if the Red Sox just won the World Series.

JOANNE
Is that it?

BRUCE
YES!

JOANNE

Thank you.

BRUCE
Yes!

JOANNE
Are you excited?

BRUCE
I am!

JOANNE
You're excited?

BRUCE
I am!

JOANNE
Bruce?

BRUCE
I promise I'm excited!

JOANNE
You should be much more excited besides the football ecstatic
scream you just did. You need to show that you are excited. You
should show that you are all excited about the fact that we…

BRUCE
You really talk too much!

Bruce grabs Joanne and kisses her. They break rather quickly

BRUCE
I'm sorry…

JOANNE
Oh…

BRUCE
I'm really sorry…

JOANNE
It's okay…

BRUCE
We're excited!

JOANNE
We are excited!

They kiss again

BRUCE
That was all me…

JOANNE
Well yea…but it's okay…

BRUCE
It's okay?

JOANNE
We are okay…

They kiss again even more passionately

MALCOLM
Okay you guys really need to get a room.

JOANNE
Oh god, Mal I'm sorry, you must hate me.

MALCOLM
I'm indifferent

JOANNE
You're indifferent?

BRUCE
Dude, I mean…

MALCOLM
Guys, honestly, it's fine, just get a room please.

JOANNE
No, I mean we went out... well we were going out…I mean I think
we are technically going out…

BRUCE
I mean best friend rule 325.

MALCOLM
203

BRUCE
Dude I'm…

MALCOLM
Guys, clearly you were meant for each other. Good or bad, hard or
easy, difficult or not difficult, guess what? You guys love each
other. When two people love each other as much as you two do,
who am I to stand in your way? Yeah, you argue and sometimes
hate each other but what couple doesn't? You think Beauty and the
Beast get along all the time? All I ask of both of you is name your

first child after me, buy a house close so I can visit, and please for the love of God, get a room!!

Bruce and Joanne hug and kiss each other.

MALCOLM
I meant a different room from here.

Sherri and Amanda enter with champagne in their hands.

SHERRI
Oh My God!

They see Bruce and Joanne making out.

AMANDA
Oh my god!

Bruce and Joanne stop what they are doing.

SHERRI
I knew it!

AMANDA
Damnit!

Amanda reaches in her pocket and hands Sherri 10 bucks.

SHERRI
Anyway, congratulations!

AMANDA
Did you see that crowd, my dear?

SHERRI

I couldn't believe it.

MALCOLM
What was the crowd doing?

SHERRI
They stood on their feet and applauded and applauded and applauded some more. They stood there applauding for 15 minutes; no other community theater production has done that!

AMANDA
Oh my God!

SHERRI
I can't believe it. It's gold, we won.

AMANDA
There were no explosions!

SHERRI
And we won!

AMANDA
No sex scenes!

SHERRI
And we won!

AMANDA
No huge special effects!

SHERRI
And we won!!

BRUCE

Except my epic death scene!

SHERRI
Yea, we should have cut that.

AMANDA
Agreed!

SHERRI
They liked the play because of the characters.

AMANDA
oh my god!

SHERRI
Come on say it!

AMANDA
What?

SHERRI
Say it!

AMANDA
No!

SHERRI
Search your feelings, you know it to be turn. Find the humble part of yourself deep inside of you and say it!

AMANDA
Okay! Fine! The boy was right!

SHERRI
Pay up!

Amanda reaches into her pocket and hands Sherri another $10.

SHERRI
You should all be proud of yourselves every one of you!

BRUCE (sing-song-y)
We did it! We did it!

AMANDA
Where is our boy?

Pat walks in a daze.

PAT
Oh my god, did you see that crowd!

ALL BUT PAT
There she is!

PAT
Did you see that crowd?

ALL BUT PAT
FOR SHE'S A JOLLY GOOD FELLA
FOR SHE'S A JOLLY GOOD FELLA
FOR SHE'S A JOLLY GOOD FELLA
WHICH NOBODY CAN DENY

PAT
Can I say something?

AMANDA
Please!

PAT

I know that maybe sometimes I have not been the easiest, calmest, or even logical collaborator but this is not just my play, this is our play. I just can't believe it. Characters and stories took that stage and that stage alone and we were able to bring that audience to their feet as if they were meant to be on their feet. All we used was words and actions. Live theater is a miracle when you can do that. I wish I could bottle that right now! Anyway, I really want to show you all how appreciative I am that you stuck with it and we did this together. Thank you!

AMANDA

A toast, we must have a toast, my kingdom for a toast!
SHERRI
let's pour the champagne!

They all get some champagne.

AMANDA

But let's not allow this to diminish what we will do in the future; we have seven more performances that need to be equally good. A toast will be good to our production to our cast, your director, producer to say nothing of the fact that this whole thing would not be possible without out magic man over there. Thank you, Aristophanes, for shinning down upon us and please shine upon us next time.

They all drink except Pat.

AMANDA

well my boy, I must be off, but I'll wait to hear from you.

She goes to shake her hand, Pat hugs her.

PAT

Thank you

AMANDA
Great job, my man

PAT
Amanda, I hate to correct you but I'm a woman.

AMANDA
Ha! Put that in your next play, my boy! Now you (to Malcolm) you are currently single, yes?

MALCOLM
Apparently…

AMANDA
Well how about I make you into a man?

MALCOLM
I'm just catnip to the ladies.

AMANDA
Avante!!! (exits with Malcolm)

BRUCE
Let's go to a bar, I'm buying,

SHERRI
You have a show tomorrow.

BRUCE
She's right, no shots.

JOANNE
You are impossible.

BRUCE
Come on, say it!

JOANNE
What?

BRUCE
Say it!

JOANNE
Ugh…I love you…

BRUCE
I can't hear you!

JOANNE
I love you!

BRUCE
I fucking knew it! And I marginally tolerate you!

JOANNE
What?!

BRUCE
I'm kidding, I love you very much!

They kiss...

JOANNE
Should I bring the whip?

They exit together.

SHERRI

Well, is it your show now?

PAT

No, and it's not really ours, it's the audiences

SHERRI

No, it's always your show, it is your show.

They hug

SHERRI

Thank you

PAT

Thank you, Sherri.

SHERRI

I'll…I'll want to hear from you soon about your next project.

PAT

My next project?

SHERRI

Yea, your next project, I want you to write another play. The theater wants you to write another play. Clearly the audience wants you to write another play.

PAT

You mean?

SHERRI

You got your commission…

PAT

Really?

SHERRI
Yes.

PAT
Really?

SHERRI
Yes!

PAT
Really?

SHERRI
Yes, and we can get another director and cast if you want, how about…

PAT
No, same cast, same director next time around, it worked. You were right.

SHERRI
I was hoping you'd say that (starts to leave)

PAT
Can you just make sure Amanda knows I'm a woman?

SHERRI
She's very stubborn…

PAT
Oh, by the way, here you go (hands Sherri a bunch of papers).

SHERRI

What's this?

PAT
Your notes

SHERRI
What?

PAT
These are the notes you gave me on my play. The last draft before
we opened addressed them all.

SHERRI
Wow…Thank you.

PAT
You still think it was a waste of time?

SHERRI
No, and my husband would have been proud, thank you. (smiles
and exits).

*Pat stands for a second and goes back to her desk. She opens a
notebook an takes up a pen, she thinks for a second and then a
worried look comes to her.*

PAT
No! I don't have any new ideas…

Lights out

Curtain down/Bows

THE END

ACKNOWLEDGEMENTS
First of all, I have to thank my wife, Megan who not only edited this collection and
helped me put this whole thing together but has had the enthusiasm and patience to
support and help me in my career as a playwright and a director. To say that she has
sacrificed much is the world's biggest understatement. I don't think that when we got
married that she would have imagined such a life like ours. Sometimes unpredictable and
sometimes difficult, mostly because of my doing, but the fact that she has continued to
support me and never once discouraged me or my career, she's a saint. I wouldn't be
anywhere close to where I am and have the confidence I have if it wasn't for her.

I need to also thank my mother. She introduced me to theater at such a young age and got
me hooked immediately. She does have a realistic approach to life and wanted to make
sure, I had a good job and could support my family, but she has been to every show I
have directed and most of the shows that I actually wrote. She was my first and original
cheerleader and when she says to me that she is very proud of me then I don't think
there's an award out there that I could get that would make me feel more accomplished
than that.

I do want to thank my father. He was never really big on the whole me being a part of

theater and creative worlds when I could be making a living and supporting my family in
more commercial and financially satisfying ways but I do hope he realizes how much
material he has given me over the years and I honestly hope that I made him proud.

A Big Thank you of course to the original cast who brought these characters to live but
also helped with the development of the characters and the various rewrites even after the
original production.

Also, a big thank you to Acting out Company for taking a chance on
this play and allowing it to be on their stage.

A big thank you to Jodie Putnam who directed the first version and definitely helped with the development and brought her own spin to the production and made the first version a huge success.

ABOUT THE AUTHOR
Matthew Garlin Author
His acting credits include Quannapowitt Players: *Suburban Holidays 3, 4, 5 & 6* and *A Midsummer Night's Dream*, Theatre to Go: *Arsenic and Old Lace* and *Twelfth Night*, New England School of Performing Arts: *The Breakfast Club* and The Bard Brigade: *The Tempest, The Merchant of Venice,* and *Macbeth*, Revolutionary Theatre: *Shakespeare Academy*, Still Small theatre's repertory company for *How I Met Our Father* and *The Diary of Perpetua*. His directing credits include *Enchanted April* for Theatre to Go Inc., Almost *Maine* and *It's a Wonderful Life* for Theater Company of Saugus, *Godspell* for Sherwood Entertainment, *Side by Side by Sondheim* for Colonial Chorus Players, *Twelfth Night* for The Bard Brigade, and a short film *Project Invisible*. His playwright credits include: *Online Dating (one act play)* and *Curtain Call (Full length play)* at Acting Out Company in Lawrence, *How Do You Know (one act play)* at River's Edge Arts Alliance, *Woods (full length play)* at Theater@First, and *A Christmas Gift (one act play)* at Theater company of Saugus. His composer credits include: *Almost Maine* for Theater Company of Saugus, *Macbeth*, and *Much Ado About Nothing* for The Bard Brigade *Enchanted April* for Theatre to Go.